Forgive
and
Forget

The Story of Joseph

Written and Illustrated by
Damon J. Taylor

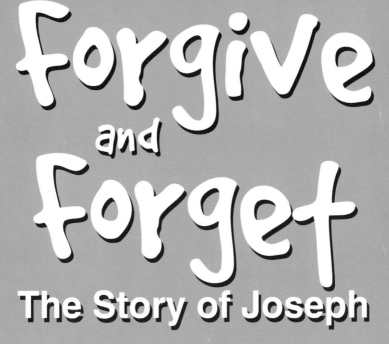

KREGEL
Kidzone

FOR PARENTS
with Dr. Sock

This story will help children learn about forgiveness. All siblings have squabbles, but Joseph and his brothers really had trouble!

Read It Together–

The story of Joseph and his brothers appears in the Old Testament book of Genesis, chapters 37–47. The story of how Joseph's brothers treated him, and how he responded, is interwoven throughout these eleven chapters.

Sharing–

Share with your child about a time when you were forgiven something. Then tell about a time you forgave someone yourself. Your children need to know that you've done things that required forgiveness, and that you're ready to forgive them.

Discussion Starters–

• Should Coleman have forgiven Shelby? Why?

• What is something you've needed forgiveness for?

• Do you think all the brothers agreed on how to treat Joseph?

• What are some of the things Joseph did that impressed his masters?

• How does it make you feel to forgive someone? How does it make you feel to be forgiven?

For Fun–

Give your kids "camel back" rides through the "desert." What would be the best thing about riding on camels? What would be the worst thing?

Draw–

Make your own "coats of many colors." Be creative! Use chalk or construction paper or glitter and markers or crayons or a little bit of everything!

Prayer Time–

Thank God for forgiving us no matter what we do, and ask Him to help us forgive each other.

COLEMAN HAS FOUND THAT THE LIFE OF A LITTLE BOY

can be tough at times, especially if that boy has a baby sister named Shelby. When Shelby was born, Coleman needed a way to deal with his day-to-day problems. He found his socks. Yes, that's right, his socks.

It may seem weird, but these aren't your regular, everyday tube socks that you find in your dresser. As ordinary as they may appear, these socks really are Coleman's friends, and they help him with his problems. When life gets complicated, Coleman goes to his bedroom and works through his troubles by playing make-believe with his socks and remembering Bible stories he's learned.

So please sit back, take off your shoes and socks if you like, and enjoy Coleman's imaginary world in . . .

forgive and forget
The Story of Joseph

One day, Coleman couldn't find his pile of socks. "Where are you guys? Come out, come out wherever you are!"

He looked in
the laundry
room.

"Hello?"

He looked in the
kitchen. "Nope,
they're not here."

He looked in
his bedroom.
  "Ah ha! . . .
Nope."

"Where can they be?" he said.
Then he heard something.

"SHELBY, N-O-O-O!" he yelled.
"G-get my socks out of your mouth.
You're making them all slimy with baby spit!
Why are you always taking my stuff?"

"Don't ever play with my socks again! I'm never gonna forgive you for this!" Coleman took his socks from Shelby, and she started to cry.

"Oh, great! Now you're bawling."

Coleman grabbed his soggy socks from
Shelby and ran off to his bedroom to sulk.

Coleman was angry. He slumped down on his bedroom floor and was picking through his soggy socks when he heard a voice.

"Coleman, why were you so mean to Shelby?" It was Sockariah, one of Coleman's play socks.

The sock hopped to the top of the pile, and asked Coleman, "Why did you hurt her feelings? She's just a baby! She didn't mean to hurt anything. Do you remember the story of Joseph and his mean brothers?"

Coleman shook his head no.

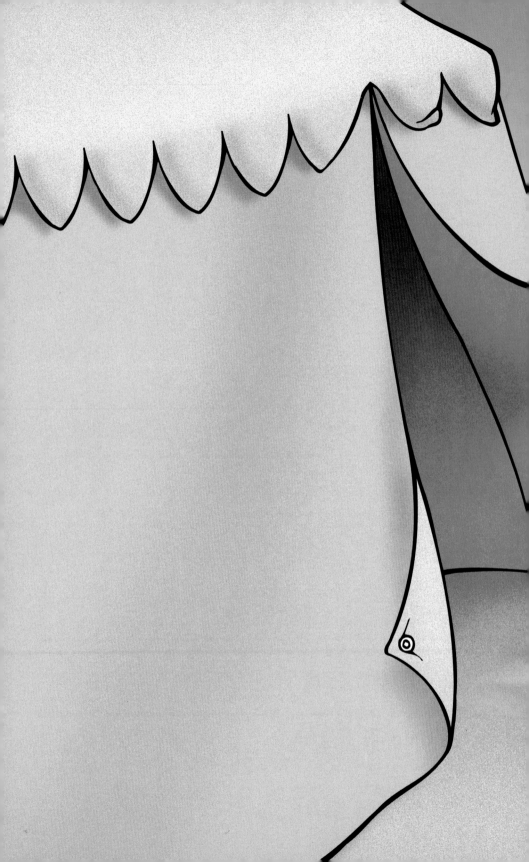

Joseph's father, Jacob, gave him a beautiful coat of many colors.

"Wow, Dad! Thanks!" said Joseph as he tried it on. "It fits perfectly! Hey, I think I'll run and show my brothers my new coat." Joseph was very excited.

Out in the pasture, where they were tending sheep, Joseph's brothers saw him coming.

"Here he comes, daddy's little dreamer boy!" said one of his brothers.

"What the . . . Hey, what's he wearing?!" said another.

"Looks like he's got a new coat," said the third brother, "and I'll bet he's coming to show it off."

"I hate it when he shows off," said another brother. "Wouldn't it be great if something terrible would happen to him?"

Reuben, the oldest brother, didn't want to see Joseph get hurt. He had an idea that might save Joseph's life.

"Hi, guys. What's up?" asked Joseph as he arrived at his brothers' campsite.

"You are!" they yelled as they picked him up and carried him off.

"Hey, take it easy. You're wrinkling my new coat!" said Joseph. "Careful fellas, you're getting close to that open piiiiiittt!" cried Joseph as his brothers stripped off his new coat and threw him into a pit.

A caravan of slave traders happened to be passing by, and Joseph's brothers saw their chance to get rid of their bragging brother—forever. They pulled Joseph out of the pit and sold him to the slave traders. Joseph was now a slave headed for a faraway land called Egypt.

The slave traders sold Joseph at the the Egyptian
sockmarket, down at the sock exchange.

"Oh, that's bad," said Coleman.

"That's nothing. It gets even worse," said Sockariah.

Joseph was sold to an Egyptian named Potiphar.

"Who's he?" asked Coleman.

"Potiphar was an officer in Pharaoh's court."

"Pharaoh had a tennis court?"

"No, Coleman, not a tennis court. Pharaoh was the king of Egypt, and kings hold court at the palace, and . . . Oh, never mind!"

Joseph worked hard for Potiphar. He quickly became Potiphar's favorite slave, and was put in charge of many things. Life as a slave was going pretty well for Joseph, until Potiphar's wife wanted Joseph to be her boyfriend.

Joseph said, "No! I am loyal to Potiphar, your husband." Because Joseph said no, she had Joseph arrested and thrown into prison.

While Joseph was in jail, he—

"Let me guess," said Coleman. "He worked hard and became the prison's favorite prisoner."

"Yep. And Joseph made some friends in prison, too. One friend was the king's baker and another was the king's cup-bearer. Well, they had been, anyway," Sockariah continued, "but now they were just prisoners."

One morning the baker said, "I had the weirdest dream last night."

"Me too," said the cup-bearer. "What was *your* dream about?"

The baker and the cup-bearer talked about their dreams as Joseph listened. When they had finished, God revealed to Joseph what their dreams meant, and Joseph told them.

PRISONER of the MONTH

"Your dream, Mr. Cup-Bearer, means that you will soon have your old job back." This news made the man very happy.

"I'm sorry, Mr. Baker, but your dream means that soon you will no longer have a place to wear your puffy chef's hat."

What Joseph said about their dreams came true,
which was a sad thing for Mr. Baker.

When the cup-bearer left the prison, Joseph called
out to him, "Don't forget me when you are working
for Pharaoh."

"I won't," promised the cup-bearer.
But he quickly *did* forget Joseph.

Months passed. One night, Pharaoh had not one but two dreams. He demanded that his wise men explain his dreams to him, but none of them could tell him what the dreams meant. From the back of the room, Pharaoh heard . . .

"Oh, yeah . . . I completely forgot!"

The king's cup-bearer had just remembered that Joseph was still in jail and that Joseph could help Pharaoh understand his dreams. Quick as a flash, Joseph was standing in front of Pharaoh, explaining Pharaoh's dreams.

Joseph said, "Your dreams mean that for seven years there will be lots of food, but the following seven years will bring a great famine. So it might be a good idea to start preparing for the bad years now."

Pharaoh was pleased with Joseph. Who do you think he put in charge of all of Pharaoh's kingdom? You guessed it . . . Joseph. Joseph quickly became Pharaoh's favorite servant.

Time passed, and the seven years of famine came.
One day, Joseph saw some people standing in line for
food. Joseph's heart sank, and his eyes filled with
tears. His ten brothers were waiting in the line.

Joseph wondered what he should do. Should he
have them arrested and thrown in jail for what they
did to him?

REMEMBER, JUST
GIVE YOUR ORDER,
STEP TO THE LEFT,
AND DON'T MAKE EYE
CONTACT!

TAKE
A
NUMBER

He knew that wasn't what God would have him do. Joseph gave his brothers food and after sending more food back to his family, he revealed his true identity. He was Joseph, their long lost brother. Joseph forgave his brothers and invited all his family to come and live in Egypt.

"Wow, I love that story," said Coleman.

"What did you learn from it?" asked Sockariah.

"Well, . . . I think . . . I think it would be great to be God's favorite, like Joseph was."

"Yeah. Anything else?"

"I . . . I also learned that God wants me to forgive Shelby for chewing up my socks. Just like Joseph forgave his brothers."

"You know, I think I'm gonna give her one of my socks right now."

"Great idea, Coleman . . . as long as the sock you give her isn't *me*," said Sockariah as he slowly backed away from Coleman.

"Cole, old buddy . . . Coleman?!!"

The Child Sockology Series

For ages up to 5
Bible Characters A to Z
Bible Numbers 1 to 10
Bible Opposites
New Testament Bible Feelings

For ages 5 and up
The Ark and the Park: The Story of Noah
Beauty and the Booster: The Story of Esther
Forgive and Forget: The Story of Joseph
Hide and Sink: The Story of Jonah